I'm Going To R

These levels are meant only as guides;
you and your child can best choose a book that's right.

Level 1: Kindergarten–Grade 1 . . . Ages 4–6
- word bank to highlight new words
- consistent placement of text to promote readability
- easy words and phrases
- simple sentences build to make simple stories
- art and design help new readers decode text

Level 2: Grade 1 . . . Ages 6–7
- word bank to highlight new words
- rhyming texts introduced
- more difficult words, but vocabulary is still limited
- longer sentences and longer stories
- designed for easy readability

Level 3: Grade 2 . . . Ages 7–8
- richer vocabulary of up to 200 different words
- varied sentence structure
- high-interest stories with longer plots
- designed to promote independent reading

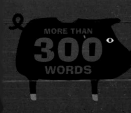

Level 4: Grades 3 and up . . . Ages 8 and up
- richer vocabulary of more than 300 different words
- short chapters, multiple stories, or poems
- more complex plots for the newly independent reader
- emphasis on reading for meaning

LEVEL 2

Library of Congress Cataloging-in-Publication Data Available

2 4 6 8 10 9 7 5 3 1

Published by Sterling Publishing Co., Inc.
387 Park Avenue South, New York, NY 10016
Text copyright © 2006 by Harriet Ziefert Inc.
Illustrations copyright © 2006 by Sanford Hoffman
Distributed in Canada by Sterling Publishing
c/o Canadian Manda Group, 165 Dufferin Street
Toronto, Ontario, Canada M6K 3H6
Distributed in Great Britain and Europe by Chris Lloyd at Orca Book
Services, Stanley House, Fleets Lane, Poole BH15 3AJ, England
Distributed in Australia by Capricorn Link (Australia) Pty. Ltd.
P.O. Box 704, Windsor, NSW 2756, Australia

Sterling ISBN 13: 978-1-4027-3680-3
Sterling ISBN 10: 1-4027-3680-0

For information about custom editions, special sales, premium and
corporate purchases, please contact Sterling Special Sales
Department at 800-805-5489 or specialsales@sterlingpub.com.

TOO MUCH TOOTING!

Pictures by Sanford Hoffman

Sterling Publishing Co., Inc.

and music found room wanted red toote

Andy wanted to make music.
So he went to his room
and found his red horn.

Andy tooted his horn.
Toot, toot!
Toot . . . toot . . . toot!

said   Andy's   I'm

Andy's grandpa said,
  "Don't toot here!
    I'm eating."

Andy's grandma said,
"Don't toot here!
I'm reading."

"Don't toot here,"
said Andy's mom.
"You'll scare the cat."

"Don't toot here,"
said Andy's dad.
"I'm working."

working

Andy yelled,
"I can't toot near Grandpa!
I can't toot near Grandma!
I can't toot near Mom and Dad!
I can't toot near the cat!
So where can I toot?"

where   can't   can

Andy went to his room.
He shut the door and tooted.

Andy made a BIG noise.

But it was no fun.

No one could hear his music.

Andy went outside.
He wet his lips.
Then he tooted—
TOOT! TOOT!

A cat heard
Andy's toot.

TOOT!

TOOT!

A dog heard
him, too.

A little girl heard Andy.

And so did a little boy.

He said, "I'll be the bandleader.
You be the band."

"Okay," they said.

They marched
all the way
to Andy's house.

"Where have you been?"
asked Andy's mom and dad.

"I missed you," said Andy's grandma.

"We all missed you,"
said Andy's grandpa.

"Too quiet?" said Andy.
"I'll make noise."

"It gets too quiet
when you are not here."

gets   we   are